W9-BTM-631

Iris Has a Virus

Arlene Alda

Illustrated by Lisa Desimini

Tundra Books

Published in Canada by Tundra Books,
75 Sherbourne Street, Toronto, Ontario M5A 2P9

Published in the United States by Tundra Books of Northern New York,
P.O. Box 1030, Plattsburgh, New York 12901

Library of Congress Control Number: 2007938538

Library and Archives Canada Cataloguing in Publication

Alda, Arlene, 1933-
Iris has a virus / Arlene Alda ; illustrated by Lisa Desimini.

For ages 4-7.
ISBN 978-0-88776-844-6

1. Viruses – Juvenile fiction. I. Desimini, Lisa II. Title.

PZ7.A358Ir 2008 j813'.54 C2007-906101-X

We acknowledge the financial support of the Government of Canada through the Book Publishing Industry Development Program (BPIDP) and that of the Government of Ontario through the Ontario Media Development Corporation's Ontario Book Initiative.
We further acknowledge the support of the Canada Council for the Arts and the Ontario Arts Council for our publishing program.

ONTARIO ARTS COUNCIL
CONSEIL DES ARTS DE L'ONTARIO

Medium: Cut-paper collage and digital

Printed in China

1 2 3 4 5 6 13 12 11 10 09 08

For Alan ...
a kid at heart
A.A.
For Violet
and Ellis
L.D.

ris' best friends in class were absent.

Jake was out and so was Sam,
Ellie, too, along with Pam.

Mrs. Morgan had said, "There's a nasty stomach virus going around. Wash your hands well, especially when you get home from school."

At home, Iris washed her hands, but something was not quite right. Iris felt tired. Very tired.

In bed –

She tried to read her storybook,
but fell asleep before a look

at even the first page.

The next morning, Iris didn't feel at all well.

"What's wrong?" asked her twin brother, Doug.

"Remember, last night, when I didn't feel right?

Well, today I'm worse," said Iris sadly.

"How are we supposed to go to Grandpa's party this Saturday?

I guess that you care, but it's just not fair

that you get sick when we're supposed to have fun," said Doug.

A large tear ran down Iris' cheek.

Mom said, "Of course Iris cares. How would you feel if she blamed you for being sick?"

Most of Thursday, Iris stayed in bed. She was too tired to read. She was too tired to watch TV. And using her new sketchbook was simply out of the question. Iris felt exhausted.

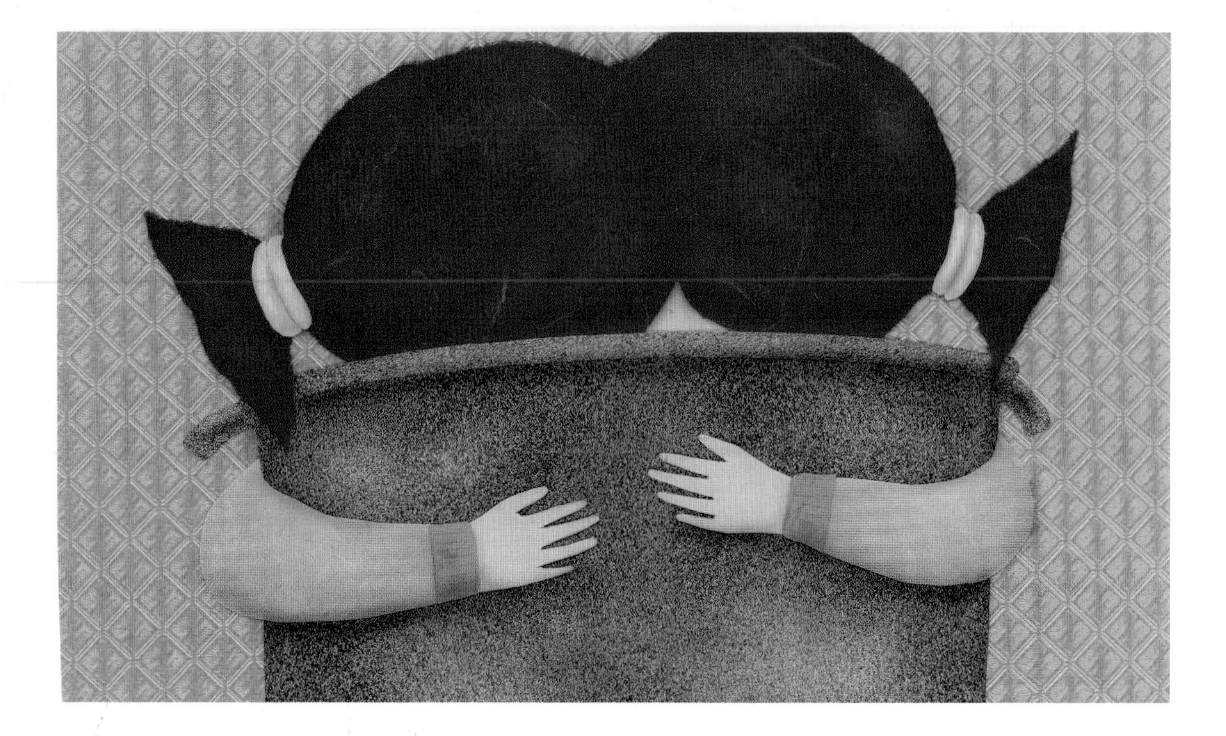

On Friday, while Doug went to school, Iris stayed home, still sick.

Her head was hot.
She threw up in a pot.

Mom said to Iris, "Let's see Dr. Sally.

We'll go in the car.
It's not very far."

In the doctor's office, Mom and Iris waited their turn.

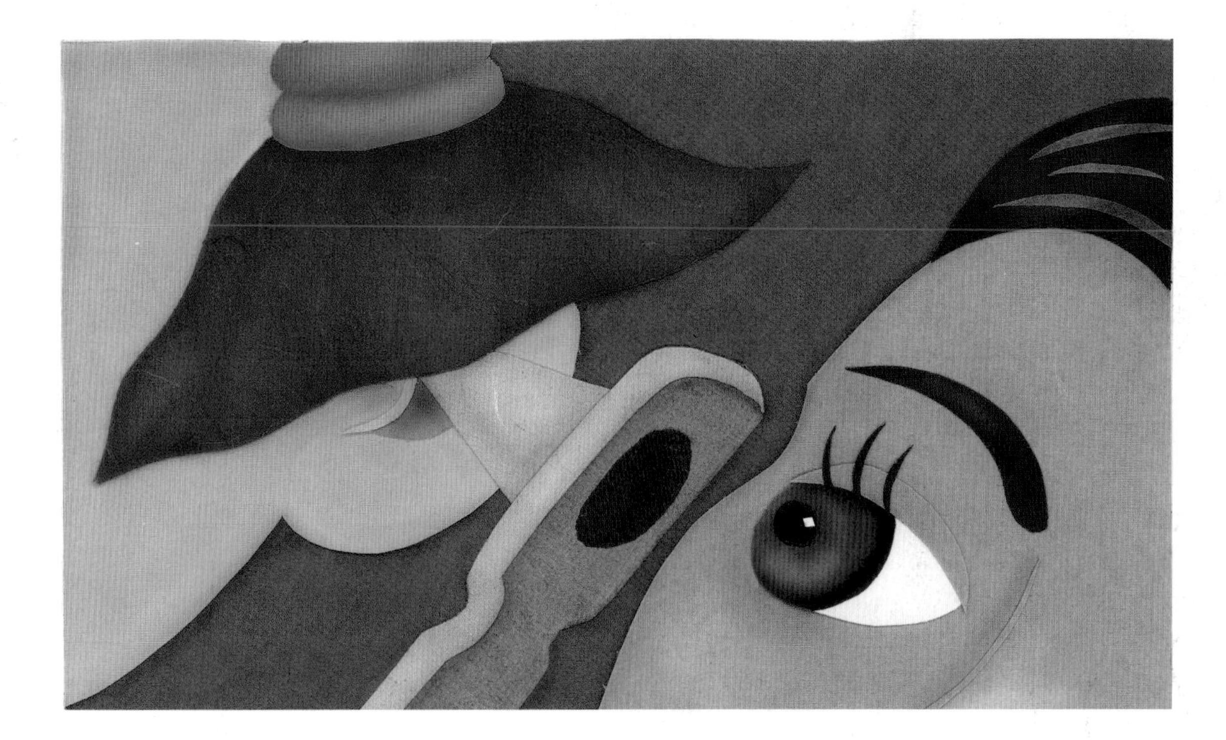

Dr. Sally listened to Iris' heart with a stethoscope. Then she looked in her mouth.

"*Ahhhhhh,*" Iris said.
Her throat wasn't red.

Dr. Sally pressed Iris' tummy and looked in her ears.

"You're looking sad.
It's not so bad.

I think you're OK, except for a virus. A nasty bug that's on its way out," she said.

At home, Iris' dreams were of bugs:

Bugs with spots,
Bugs on cots,
Bugs like ants,
Bugs with pants.

Bugs on a train,
Bugs in the rain,
Bugs that could walk,
Bugs that could talk.

Red bugs, blue ones,
White ones, too.
Bugs that could drink,
Bugs that could chew.

Iris woke up on Saturday feeling much better. She told Doug, Mom, and Dad about her dreams of bugs.

"A virus is a special kind of bug," said Dad. "It's a germ. You see it through a magnifier called a microscope."

Iris thought for a moment. *My bug is gone.*

If that's so,
where did it go?

Iris felt well enough to go to Grandpa's party.

They got in the car
and didn't go far,

when Doug got awfully quiet.

"I don't feel well," he said.
"Will you feel my head?"

Dad stopped the car and felt Doug's head.

Doug's head was hot.
He threw up a lot.

"Well," said Mom and Dad,

"Iris had a virus ...
and now Doug has her bug."

Iris looked at Mom and Dad. "Can't we go anyway ... and have Doug stay home with a sitter?" she asked, a grin on her face.

Iris looked at Mom and Dad. "Can't we go anyway ... and have Doug stay home with a sitter?" she asked, a grin on her face.